PRAISE FOR M. L. BUCHMAN

(Miranda Chase is) one of the most compelling, addicting, fascinating characters in any genre since the Monk television series.

— DRONE, ERNEST DEMPSEY

The first...of (a) stellar, long-running (military) romantic suspense series.

— THE NIGHT IS MINE, BOOKLIST, THE 20 BEST
ROMANTIC SUSPENSE NOVELS: MODERN
MASTERPIECES

Buchman has catapulted his way to the top tier of my favorite authors.

— FRESH FICTION

M L. Buchman's ability to keep the reader right in the middle of the action is amazing.

— LONG AND SHORT REVIEWS

The only thing you'll ask yourself is, "When does the next one come out?"

— WAIT UNTIL MIDNIGHT, ROMANTIC TIMES BOOK
REVIEWS, 4 STARS

I knew the books would be good, but I didn't realize how good.

— NIGHT STALKERS SERIES, KIRKUS REVIEWS

DREAMS OF CRYSTAL

A SCIENCE FICTION ROMANCE

M. L. BUCHMAN

Buchman Bookworks

SIGN UP FOR M. L. BUCHMAN'S NEWSLETTER TODAY

and receive:
Release News
Free Short Stories
a Free book

Get your free book today. Do it now.
free-book.mlbuchman.com

Other works by M. L. Buchman: *(* - also in audio)*

Thrillers

Dead Chef
Swap Out!
One Chef!
Two Chef!

Miranda Chase
*Drone**
*Thunderbolt**
*Condor**

Romantic Suspense

Delta Force
*Target Engaged**
*Heart Strike**
*Wild Justice**
*Midnight Trust**

Firehawks
MAIN FLIGHT
Pure Heat
Full Blaze
*Hot Point**
*Flash of Fire**
Wild Fire
SMOKEJUMPERS
*Wildfire at Dawn**
*Wildfire at Larch Creek**
*Wildfire on the Skagit**

The Night Stalkers
MAIN FLIGHT
The Night Is Mine
I Own the Dawn
Wait Until Dark
Take Over at Midnight
Light Up the Night
Bring On the Dusk
By Break of Day

AND THE NAVY
Christmas at Steel Beach
Christmas at Peleliu Cove
WHITE HOUSE HOLIDAY
*Daniel's Christmas**
*Frank's Independence Day**
*Peter's Christmas**
*Zachary's Christmas**
*Roy's Independence Day**
*Damien's Christmas**
5E
Target of the Heart
Target Lock on Love
Target of Mine
Target of One's Own

Shadow Force: Psi
*At the Slightest Sound**
*At the Quietest Word**

White House Protection Force
*Off the Leash**
*On Your Mark**
*In the Weeds**

Contemporary Romance

Eagle Cove
Return to Eagle Cove
Recipe for Eagle Cove
Longing for Eagle Cove
Keepsake for Eagle Cove

Henderson's Ranch
*Nathan's Big Sky**
*Big Sky, Loyal Heart**
*Big Sky Dog Whisperer**

Love Abroad
Heart of the Cotswolds: England
Path of Love: Cinque Terre, Italy

Other works by M. L. Buchman:

Contemporary Romance (cont)

Where Dreams
Where Dreams are Born
Where Dreams Reside
Where Dreams Are of Christmas
Where Dreams Unfold
Where Dreams Are Written

Science Fiction / Fantasy

Deities Anonymous
Cookbook from Hell: Reheated
Saviors 101

Single Titles
The Nara Reaction
Monk's Maze
the Me and Elsie Chronicles

Non-Fiction

Strategies for Success
Managing Your Inner Artist/Writer
Estate Planning for Authors*
Character Voice
Narrate and Record Your Own
Audiobook*

Short Story Series by M. L. Buchman:

Romantic Suspense

Delta Force
Delta Force

Firehawks
The Firehawks Lookouts
The Firehawks Hotshots
The Firebirds

The Night Stalkers
The Night Stalkers
The Night Stalkers 5E
The Night Stalkers CSAR
The Night Stalkers Wedding Stories

US Coast Guard
US Coast Guard

White House Protection Force
White House Protection Force

Contemporary Romance

Eagle Cove
Eagle Cove

Henderson's Ranch
Henderson's Ranch*

Where Dreams
Where Dreams

Thrillers

Dead Chef
Dead Chef

Science Fiction / Fantasy

Deities Anonymous
Deities Anonymous

Other
The Future Night Stalkers
Single Titles

ABOUT THIS STORY

Mavall knows his role in life: best friend to the great Dreymond Valenki—the most powerful man on the Pacific Rim.

But when they travel together into the crystal caverns of Luna seeking answers, their paths diverge.

Rediscovering the past permanently alters the paths of Drey, Mavall, and the woman they both love as they seek to understand the dreams of crystal.

1

———

"Welcome to the Crystal Caverns. We're two kilometers below the massive Tycho Crater—the greatest asteroid blow to ever strike the Moon. Never in all your days..."

Dreymond tuned out the vendor's pitch though others stopped to listen.

Drey had already done the SR walk-through. Heard the vendor state that a Sensorium Reality walk-through could never capture the true wonder but had continued the tour. Both in SR and now in reality—which tried to explain the caverns' formation and contents that no one had ever been able to explain.

Spew out enough words and the tourists might feel as if the vendor knew something, even though it was soon clear that he didn't know any more than a brochure's worth.

"Earth, Mars, or Moon, they're always selling you something." Mavall's cheery rejoinder fit Dreymond's own way of thinking. Or would have as little as six months ago.

Prima had come for a visit to the Lunar Crystal Caverns with her sister and brother—tritely named Secundo and

Tritium. Their parents might as well have chosen Hydrogen, Helium, and Lithium. Apparently they had so little sophistication they hadn't even realized they'd chosen two different dead languages—Europe had imploded economically back in the 2020s and never recovered—which actually almost made some degree of sense with Tritium being named for a nuclear fusion precursor.

None of which had dimmed Prima's light.

Atypically long, elegant, and sophisticated for someone tracing her roots back to the native Siberian tribes, she'd been a fantastic lover and a joy to live with as a bonus. He'd finally coaxed her to agree to discuss a long-term contract, after she returned from her trip.

But the woman who had left was somehow shifted by her vacation on Luna.

I'm...different inside, Dreymond, she tried to explain. She'd always refused to use his nickname of Drey—as if needing to keep a little distance. *There's... I don't know, Dreymond. I want...something different. It's not about you. You're wonderful.*

Last thing a guy ever wanted to hear. *It's not you, it's me, but go the hell away.*

Not that he'd ever heard it before from any lover he chose. But now that he had, it was worse than someone screaming at him as *she* walked out of *his* life—which also had never happened. Women usually faded for him until he didn't even notice their eventual departure.

Prima hadn't given him "the speech" yet, but he could feel it coming.

They had been like two nearly parallel mag-lev transports coming together, easing ever closer. Just when they were ready to merge onto the same track, he'd discovered there was no switch at the junction. Now their tracks had crossed, at the closest point he'd ever been with any woman, and were easing apart. The further she drifted, the more he realized quite how good he'd had it.

"Why did you drag me here again?" Mavall must be teasing.

Drey often had trouble telling with Mavall. It was impossible not to be awed by the caverns.

Discovered just five years before, the vast subterranean void was the only significant seismic anomaly discovered by the 2091 Whole Moon Survey. The rumors of black monoliths lurking beneath the lunar soil had finally been put to rest.

But in a display of irony, the caverns were in almost the exact location depicted in the ninety-year-old vid. Their vast reaches had long since been sealed and pressurized, but the full extent had yet to be completely explored. The surveyors swore the dimensions kept changing, but no one had been able to prove that.

Drey wondered if it was the nature of the caverns themselves that limited exploration—because they were big, but not that big. He'd expected to stride in and be awed. The SR pitch had certainly said he would be.

Millions, some said billions of crystals lined every even marginally horizontal surface. The walls and distant cavern roof were rough lunar rock, but that wasn't worth notice.

The true spectacle here was formed by the crystals. Some smooth and small enough to fill just the curve of the palm, others large and jagged, but still no bigger than a person's open hand. Paths had been formed among the crystals, apparently by heaping them to either side. Yet though they lay in great mounds, he impossibly felt that he could see each unique one. Clearly and distinctly.

"We're here," he told Mavall, unsure whether or not he

was rising to the bait, "because maybe I'll see here whatever Prima saw. Maybe it will bring us back together."

"Before she's wholly done with your sorry self and gone. You were never tedious about a woman before, Drey. What's with this one?"

Drey shoved Mavall into a pile of crystals. They fell, rattled, shifted, but none broke—the ad-ware said they couldn't be. Some let off bright, cheery tinkling sounds. Others dull tones. This one sounded like music, that one like a choir. A small one sounded like a tiny rocket's roar, back when they were still screwing up Earth's atmosphere by burning chemical rocketry.

Maybe it wasn't the cave's vastness that had left them only partially explored. Perhaps it was that with each step, Drey found himself moving slower. Everywhere he looked, he wanted to pick up a crystal and stare into it.

Others were doing that.

There were scores, perhaps hundreds of people wandering through the caverns at this moment—but so spread out, he could mostly exclude them from his thoughts. Every now and then someone would pick up a crystal, sometimes carrying it for a while, sometimes nervously setting it down.

Mavall began juggling several of the crystals. Was that how he dealt with the awe of this place, or did he simply not see it? The sheer volume of them made Drey want to stuff his hands in his pockets and cower like a little boy awaiting judgement for his sins.

In contrast to Drey, who overthought everything, Mavall wasn't much of a thinker. Not even as a boy when they'd met on the first day of primer school.

Mavall had been his wingman in a schoolyard game of bandy ball. Hooked sticks like hockey sticks, a knotted ball the size of his father's fist—something he had the occasion to know the exact size of. And Mavall's perfect pass had let him score the winning goal at the same time it sealed their friendship.

They'd been close ever since.

Also around him, Drey didn't have to try overly hard. There was no judgement about his grades, his career, his occasional need to binge-watch an entire bandy tournament —Mavall was simply a friend he could count on.

Even as Mavall juggled them, each crystal seemed to wink at Drey. Without glowing in any detectable way, the entire cavern was lit by their light, pale and bright, red and violet and every color in between. Still...

He wandered farther along one of the lanes cleared of crystals.

Mavall followed in his wake.

"There are stories about these, you know?" Mavall was down to a single crystal, tossing it hand to hand in glittering arcs that reached ten, twenty, thirty meters high in the light gravity. When his aim was off he'd do a lunge knee- or even thigh-deep off the path's crystal-piled borders to catch it. No one came to warn him off, so it must be okay. Or they knew better than to interfere with a companion of Dreymond Valenki.

"What stories?"

2

MAVALL CAUGHT THE CRYSTAL CLEAN AFTER ITS HIGHEST ARC yet—still not reaching the cavern's ceiling. He kept meaning to let the crystal drop, see for himself whether or not it broke on impact. But each time, he found himself reluctant to take the risk.

Also, if it did fall to the side, it might get mixed in with the others and he'd never see it again.

He liked this crystal. The smooth feel against his palm. The slight pulsing warmth. It made him think of a woman's thigh. Not during sex—the way he'd usually think of it—but after, when it was draped lazily over his hips and his hand rested so that he could just feel the pulse ticking away behind her knee. A time bomb, or a timing of some passage anyway, that eased back from the explosion of release until it drifted as lightly as an ocean wave...or a crystal falling through air under lunar gravity.

"You know that they sell these? The guys who first cored down here and pressurized it."

"Hard to miss," Drey waved a hand back at the vendor who was calling his pitch at a new set of arrivals.

"They say that no one buys more than one. And anyone who buys one, never shows it to anyone else."

"Who the hell are *they?*" Drey always asked things like that.

Mavall never cared. *They* was good enough for most people, why not good enough for Drey? It seemed nothing ever was.

Vinka hadn't done it for him.

Nor Melafane.

And now he was losing Prima. At least he was fighting for her enough to come here. Not his usual style, but past experience didn't bode well for his friend.

"These are stories, okay? I hear things. You never listen." Another thing Drey had never been strong on.

"I never have to. You listen to everything, then you always tell me what I need to know even if I don't want to hear it."

Mavall tossed his crystal. Less high now. Less chance of it going astray.

Was that his role? Translator of the world at large to the great Dreymond Valenki? Didn't sound like as much fun as it should. Drey was old money and old status reaching all the way back to the Chinese Fracture. In the three ugly years it had taken the People's Republic to break into seven countries—of which four had mostly starved to death—the Valenki Clan had run south out of Vladivostok buying most of Nanjing at rock bottom prices. By then Shanghai and the other coastal provinces had been underwater and were little more than a shipping hazard to the new Valenki stronghold.

Drey wasn't his patron, but Mavall wasn't sure quite what he was either. Perhaps the closest thing Drey had to a friend? Outside of their friendship, Drey was always conscious of his image and his position as the presumptive heir of the Valenki financial empire.

Prima Markova was been perfect in the role of companion. What the Valenkis wielded in financial heft, the Markova Clan wielded in social power. Together Drey and Prima would be formidable. She'd always struck Mavall as something of an icy bitch, yet there was a magnetism to her dark perfection that was impossible to ignore. And sometimes there were hints that she was laughing—even if no one else got the joke.

That one little glimpse of her intrigued him more than it should for his best friend's lover.

"So why do *they* think that is?" Drey prompted him.

"Why what is?" If Drey wanted it, he was damn well going to have to earn it.

"Mavall," he lowered his voice—about as close as he ever came to anger. Mavall had seen him cow entire boardrooms with that tone. But Mavall had helped him practice the tone after his voice change and knew better than to be scared of it.

"Why should I tell you?"

Drey studied him in some surprise.

Mavall knew he was the spineless one of their friendship —supposedly. Drey said that's why he kept Mavall around. But Mavall knew better. He was Drey's embodied patience. Able to joke him out of bad moods and keep the head-in-everything-but-name of the Valenki Empire functioning well.

Well, Mavall wasn't feeling as much patience as usual. Of course, it also wasn't like Drey to care enough about something to whine about it.

"There are rumors of change."

9

"World's always changing," but Drey didn't have his heart in his riposte, so Mavall let it go.

"*They,*" Mavall waited, but Drey didn't rise to the bait. He held up his crystal like a monocle and pretended to peer up at his friend through it. Instead it seemed that he could see down into it. No, the feeling was that he could see *up* into it. As if he was suddenly looking up at something he'd never seen before but should have.

A brief whirl of vertigo swept through him like a morning rain shower. He shifted the crystal aside but didn't toss it in the air again.

"Your lovely Prima is not the only one who has returned changed. And the change doesn't happen to everyone—at least *they* don't think so. Still, there are rumors that something here can alter a person."

"Rumor. Innuendo."

"*They!*" Mavall wiggled his fingers as if he was sprinkling fairy dust over Drey.

"You're not being very convincing."

"You're not being very imaginative." And there was a truth he hadn't realized. It was another "duty" he fulfilled for Drey. He provided the imagination that his friend—so good at business—entirely lacked.

Drey continued stomping his way down the aisles without touching any of the beauty around him.

"Explain Prima." And a dark thundercloud seemed to form over Drey's head—foul enough to have other visitors clearing out of his way.

3

————

DREY WAS NEVER AT A LOSS. YET AS HE'D WALKED UP ONE PATH and down another in the great cavern, he'd never felt so...

He didn't know.

He'd never felt this way, so he didn't have a word for it.

Mavall was chattering happily away about fanciful social networks—member-only clubs exclusive to the holders of crystal. Or perhaps they were pre-packaged guiding lights left by some super race during the formation of the galaxy— as gifts for the primitives of Earth.

All Drey knew was that he didn't understand. And that was *not* a familiar feeling.

He picked up a double palmful of crystals and stared at them. The sharp jagged ones, that should slice his palm like shattered glass, felt no different than the one that could easily be mistaken for a luminous chicken egg. Hard, crystalline, yet somehow edgeless. Mavall would have some explanation, however fanciful.

There was a silvery star that Drey might have chosen as a gift for Prima—women seemed to like such pretty baubles. A large one of deepest red that would look fine on his desk

—but it would only remind him of how she'd changed. A complex form that looked like a wild geometrical proof made Mavall laugh when Drey held it up.

Mavall was always doing that.

Laughing at the oddest moments.

The two of them had no secrets—no real ones. Mavall had helped him on business deals—a little, it wasn't his strength. But Drey knew that their current social set was far more his friend's doing than his own.

Even this trip...

Maybe if you want to understand her, you should go as well. Mavall's idea.

...wasn't helping.

"Are you changing too?" He hoped not. Mavall had always been nonchalantly himself. Never aspiring, glad to enjoy the ride at Drey's side.

"I shed my skin cells as fast as the next man," Mavall kept toying with his crystal.

Half the time Drey didn't understand what his friend was talking about.

"I feel no different." Then Mavall had begun patting his hands down his body as if frisking himself.

4

———

THAT LIE PUZZLED MAVALL ALL THE WAY BACK TO EARTH.

He'd never been a collector. Drey had all the trappings of great wealth: gathering residences, every generation of elite skimmer in the garages, and stunning women. Mavall had never gathered such things.

But when the vendor had told him the high cost of the nondescript crystal, he'd paid the half of a percent of his entire wealth—more than he needed to live for a year, even without riding on Drey's coattails.

Oh, he'd made a joke of it, "Lend me a fiver, would you, Drey?"

However, when Drey had offered up his credit, Mavall had pushed him aside and paid it himself. The price had stung Mavall sorely to spend, but something about the simple pale blue crystal had been worth it.

Drey thought differently when the vendor named the price for the crystal Drey had finally selected. "Do you know how much I'm worth?"

The vendor hadn't blinked or cared. "If you don't value it, sir, why do you want it?"

Drey had tossed the shining gold crystal in the shape of a bandy ball back onto a pile with a clatter.

The vendor had merely raised an eyebrow as if asking he was sure, then turned to the next person.

"How much did you pay for that damn thing?" Drey had asked and Mavall had stuffed it out of sight.

But he could feel it. Knew that somehow, the price equaled the value.

Knew that Drey would never believe him and would toss aside Mavall's crystal as easily as he tossed aside most things.

And Mavall now knew for a fact that Prima had bought a crystal, despite the cost.

5

PRIMA MARKOVA WONDERED WHO SHE'D FORGOTTEN ABOUT when the chime sounded at her door. She never forgot a social engagement.

Or was someone so thoughtless as to arrive at her home uninvited?

Dreymond Valenki returned from his "mysterious errand"? As if her social network hadn't reported where he was going before he'd even left the atmosphere.

No. His errand boy, Mavall.

Dreymond had sent his sidekick to do what? Summon her? Discard her?

Prima wasn't sure which she'd prefer.

Dreymond was so perfect for her in so many ways. But...

That "but" had begun as a whim. Of course she'd be marrying Dreymond. He had to earn the right, but it wouldn't be hard. An alliance between the Valenki money and the Markova influence; their families could easily control the remaining stretches of the West Pacific Rim.

But lately Dreymond had become an irritant.

And sending his errand boy to—

Mavall held up a fist. A pale blue light shone through the gaps in his fingers.

She let him in cautiously.

He neither showed her his crystal, nor asked to see hers. Dreymond had asked at first out of idle curiosity. It had been a mistake to refuse. Had she shown it, he'd have said something pleasant and let it go. Now, however, he had latched onto it as the emblem of something being wrong with her and wouldn't leave the subject alone.

She'd never paid Mavall that much attention. He was soft where Dreymond was hard. Not fat, or even heavy, just...soft. And his coloring—

She recalled a long-ago comment. "Mom traces back to Finland. Her great-gran fell in love with a Siberian bureaucrat. Moving east was all that saved her from the European Implosion. I take after her." Pale blond hair and blue eyes. So different from Dreymond's darkness.

"I haven't seen this before."

Prima glanced where he was looking. Without thinking, she'd received him in her private apartment. The social gatherings she arranged were always held in the penthouse.

The grand room offered an all-directions view of Vladivostok—her building rose a thousand stories atop Eagle Nest Hill. It looked down at Golden Horn Bay, the Peter the Great Gulf to the Sea of Japan, and towered over the peaks of the mountains strung like a drapery down the spine of the Muravyov-Amursky Peninsula. Not tall enough to see Japan or the radioactive glow of the Korean Peninsula, but it felt as if it was.

Inside the grand room, the mezzanine suspended above provided large areas for dining and smaller spaces for more intimate meetings.

Five floors below, her private apartments had none of

the gold and crystal. This was where she lived. This was home.

No one came here.

"It looks like the inside of a country dacha. I like it." The morning sun, rising out of the Sea of Japan burnished warm woods and brightened brass fixtures. Good iron warmed around the planters.

Dreymond would have said something else...which finally explained why she'd never brought him here.

"What can I do for you, Mavall Rostov?"

She settled on the leather sofa, only as she crossed her legs becoming aware that she'd received him in her bathrobe. She flicked the thick terrycloth to cover her knees, but his eyes didn't follow the motion.

So that wasn't why he was here.

She knew that he found her attractive, but she'd already been with Dreymond when they first met and that had been the end of that. Besides, he had no influence, no great family—merely a bureaucrat's son. He always seemed so mild-mannered, hidden within the vast shadow cast by Dreymond Valenki, that she'd given him little notice.

Mavall's gaze instead contemplated the rising sun, though she doubted that's what his eyes were seeing.

"You paid the price."

He didn't make it a question, but she acknowledged it anyway. She'd paid a fortune for her crystal. She wasn't wealthy like Dreymond, but her riches were not confined to the ownership of this single skyscraper either.

"Did your siblings?"

She shook her head. And since, they too had begun to drift away like Dreymond.

After a long silence he turned to her. He didn't ask, *Why?*

as Dreymond would have. He knew. He understood. Even if she didn't.

Nor did he ask, *How have you changed?* which Dreymond had asked in a dozen different forms.

Instead Mavall sat in a chair across from her, three kilometers in the sky, near the top of the most expensive building in the entire Pacific Rim—except for Singapore, which had formed its entire country into a single vertical structure from which they still controlled the lion's share of international trade. Within the safety of this lofty perch, he asked the question she'd most feared.

"How is it changing *us?*"

6

—————

"I HAVE A THEORY."

Mavall stared up at the beach hut's thatched ceiling and contemplated the near tectonic shifts that had occurred along the fracture zones of his life.

Drey had moved out of his life, without leaving it.

Mavall was still Drey's translator to the world, but much more of Mavall's life had become his own. He liked Drey, was glad to keep him company, but it no longer defined the boundaries of Mavall's days. Like a fissure in the Ring of Fire, the crystal-driven change—for that's what it must be—cracked Mavall slowly open until he understood more of who he was as a person.

Drey had long since let go of Prima in frustration.

"I just don't understand you anymore." He'd swept up Krishi Yuan, the ruler of China Fracture Number Three—the former Shanghai region where a bare ten million had replaced the several hundred million who had lived there before.

"Don't ever take her to Lunar Caverns," Mavall had joked. Except perhaps it wasn't a joke.

Prima and Mavall had done no more than eat and eventually socialize together for the first six months after their trips to Luna.

When Prima had taken him to her bed, it had been the most natural thing Mavall had ever done in his life.

"What's your theory?" Prima lay curled up against him. Her long dark hair revealing red highlights from these last weeks spent playing on the beaches of Okinawa. He brushed her hair over his bare chest, enjoying the slick weight of it.

"What did you dream of as a child?"

"I don't remember."

"Try. I think it's important."

She turned her face into his shoulder. "I..."

"It's like dredging up the past out of some oceanic trench, isn't it?"

"Yes, a forgotten past is usually best left forgotten."

"Is it? I might have agreed once, but not anymore. Let me guess. Your crystal was sun-gold."

Prima's gasp answered his guess.

"You're always saying how cold you are. But not here in this sunny land."

"I dreamed of warmth. Except not quite the sun's warmth. As a girl I dreamed of..." She rubbed her palm on the center of his chest. "I dreamed of this warmth. And, yes, before you ask, there is also a hint of red in the very heart of the gold. But how did you know?"

He reached over to the small pouch he'd set upon the bedside table. He slipped his crystal free of the black velvet and let her see his Luna crystal for the first time.

"What is pale blue to you?" Prima asked him softly.

"It's not the blue so much as the shape, the feel of it. It's a life that's easy but perfect at the same time. When we were kids, Drey was never happy. A part of it was his father's belief that he could batter Drey into being a proper leader of the Valenki. But I think a part of him may have always been that way."

Mavall himself felt a desire to squirm away from that lost past. It was no easier for him than for Prima.

"I was just five or six when I decided that wasn't how I would live, and I haven't. I've been, if not happy, at least content. At first I thought this crystal was a reminder of that dream: that happiness was attainable. *Is* attainable." He slid his palm along over her shoulder and back.

"I like that idea," she whispered as gently as the dawn breeze rustling through the open window. "It fits you. You've taught me more about joy this last year than I knew existed. Far more than I ever expected to find for myself."

"I think this crystal is only half of the dream."

"Where's the other half?"

"I suspect that you have it."

"Me?" She pushed up enough to look down at him.

He tried to nod solemnly, but he'd never been able to not smile when he looked at her. Even worse, he could almost never tease her, though he kept trying. Drey was such an easy target that it wasn't a problem. With Prima, she could always see the mischievous smile, even when he was sure it was well hidden.

"Where?"

"Will you show me your crystal from the caves?"

He could see the doubts flicker across her features. Old doubts he knew, mere shadows of what she had previously presented to the world in such a way that he'd labeled her an icy bitch. Nothing could be further from the truth—now.

They had come to this beach resort as a honeymoon,

celebrating their long-term co-habitancy contract. But still they hadn't shared the last secret. The crystals.

"After a while," Mavall knew Prima always liked all the information before acting. Not the whats, like Drey, but the whys. Prima loved her whys. "I decided that my crystal and yours, were somehow, impossibly, our childhood dreams. That our lost dreams had manifested as crystals in a subterranean Lunar cavern in some way, by some technology or process we'll never understand. I figured it out because of Drey."

"I thought you said Drey didn't take a crystal."

"He didn't, but he picked one up and carried it as if he was done looking. When they told him the price, he tossed it away as if it meant nothing. They didn't try to coax him either—it was as if the vendor didn't care. Probably they don't suspect what these really are. I couldn't find my idea mentioned in any research."

"Neither could I," Prima's first indication that she'd use her skills as the most effective living expert of social and media interactions in an effort to understand the crystals. "What did Dreymond's young dream look like?"

"It was a golden bandy game ball."

Prima covered her mouth and her eyes went wide as a half laugh and half sob nearly choked her.

"I know. The poor guy. He so loved the game when we were growing up. He didn't want to be some faster-than-light explorer and roam the distant stars like most boys. He worshipped the teams, knew every score of every player in the league. His father beat him most often over his love of the simple game of bandy ball."

"His dream tried to come back to him, and he tossed it away," Prima groaned with pity. A tear slid down her cheek. She might be skilled at all social interactions, but Mavall knew that beneath that carefully trained image she showed to the world—at least to all the world except him—lay an incredibly tender heart. She was honestly sorry for the lost boy and the man grown.

And Mavall loved her for that heart.

"Oh, he would have become such a great man." She wiped at her tears.

"I know. That's why I still stay with him. Why I put up with his moods and whims. I can see the boy, I *remember* him. Even if Drey can't."

Prima kissed him for that.

"Now pull out your crystal."

She didn't hesitate this time, but fetched it and slipped it out of its custom redwood case. An insanely precious wood ever since the global warming had dried out the west coast of North America so badly that its entire length had been burned by a single unstoppable wildfire.

He took the golden crystal with its red heart from her. It was as lovely as Prima the dreaming girl must have been. No! As lovely as the woman watching him so intently *had become.*

The crystal looked soft, felt warm. It rested strangely in his palm. As if it belonged there, but also as if it was wholly foreign.

Very gently, unsure of what would happen, he placed the two crystals together.

They fit. The crystals of their dreams fit together perfectly. The gold and the blue didn't merge or blend, but neither would the two crystals be separate again.

"I guess that our dreams were made for one another," Prima ran a finger along the seam of the colors, for there no longer was a seam in the crystal.

"We didn't need a pair of crystals to tell us that, my love."

Her happy laugh confirmed that.

Later. Much later. After they had used each other's bodies as if to confirm how perfectly they fit together, Prima lay once more in the curve of his arm.

"What happens to the dreams no one recovers?" She didn't mention Drey's crystal aloud—he knew that neither of them would ever again—but he knew they were both thinking of it.

Mavall felt a shiver, just a hint of the deep ice that used to cover so much of Russia. Without the crystal, he'd never have found Prima. Or himself.

Yet he had.

And so had she.

But what about all the others?

IF YOU ENJOYED THIS, YOU'LL LOVE THE NARA REACTION

THE NARA REACTION (EXCERPT)

BERMUDA 2082

"SO, I'M DEAD, AM I?"

It was perfect. James Wirden's voice started with all the power one would expect from the World Premier, but it ended the most delicious twist of uncertainty. Bryce looked down at the nearly empty champagne glass in James' hand.

"Yes, sad for you, but true. Poisoned, if you must know. By me."

"And you dare to tell me this?" Such indignation from such a small man. He turned toward the guards, but Bryce clamped a friendly hand upon his shoulder to belay the movement. Not that it mattered, all of the guards along the line of French doors were his hand-picked staff. The bright lights from within cast their tall shadows across the stone terrace pushing back the edge of the Bermudan night. His men would stop any stragglers from the party, not that any would dare interrupt when the Premier and his mighty right-hand man were in conference. But no point in misplacing trust when one staged a coup.

"One of the many things you never properly appreciated, James, is the wonders of modern genetics.

There is a tiny little code-alterer running through your system even as we speak. Your genetic code is even now shifting at an exquisitely subtle level. When you have a massive stroke in three days, none shall grieve as much as your lieutenant. None shall take power with as much trepidation as your Right Hand." A nickname Bryce had carefully cultivated for years. Who better to be named to power than the man who knew the Premier's every intent?

The man struggled against his grasp just as pointlessly as a worm evading a short future pithed upon the hook that would send it into the fish's belly. Bryce took the champagne glass from James' nerveless hand and tipped the dregs over the broad stone seawall to splash into the eager waves below. Soon, he promised them, soon you may swallow this useless chattel as well.

The Premier's pale face twisted in such pain that for a moment Bryce feared the stroke would come too soon. He didn't have everything in place yet. Of course, he could compensate, but having the man die in his arms would not look good at all to the World Economic Council.

"You must remember to breathe, my good leader. Besides, in another few minutes you will remember none of this. Another wonder of genetics research you so despise is the revelation of how memories are stored. Your memory of these moments will shortly be erased. And when you pass on in three day's time, your Right Hand will be there, the Premier-to-be, Bryce Randall Stevens, Sr."

James patted at the beads of sweat on his brow with his small hand as he looked up at Bryce. He always backed up when they spoke so that he didn't have to crane his neck, but Bryce kept him in his place this time. The music surged through the open doors onto the broad patio. The orchestra had come back precisely on schedule drawing everyone's attention inward. He didn't want any to think his conversation with the Premier took overlong if the drug didn't take effect as planned. Of course he knew it would, it had worked perfectly on the man who'd engineered it for him.

"Do you hate me so?"

"Stupid man, what does hate have to do with anything? You're weak, James. Always were. If I hadn't pulled every single string over the last four decades, Parvati and her temple of democratic fairness would still be in power. I have used you, because you are far more presentable than I. No one expects a small, rotund man to be vicious. Therefore, there were no curious eyes as I did what you were too weak to do behind the scenes. But now you are beginning to interfere. You should never have nuked Auckland."

The little man sputtered. "I had to Bryce. You and your damned gene labs. There is a reason we outlawed that horrible knowledge. We did it. You and I. Together. When I found you were dabbling in that dark road to hell, of course I had to blow it out of existence."

"Too little, too late, James. Do you think I'd have let you drop those bombs if I wasn't ready? All you did for me was a little convenient housecleaning." Actually he'd barely gotten the chief scientists and the data clear. Less than an hour warning had let him salvage only the most essential elements. But the continuing research on the uses of the Second Human Genome Mapping Project lived on, even if the researchers families hadn't. And he'd gotten to look like the hero to the ones he had saved.

The blow of his failure took the fight out of the Premier. Bryce gave James' shoulder a jovial shake in show for any who might be watching.

"On December 24th, three days after this birthday party,

lovingly thrown by your second-in-command, I shall mourn at your side. I shall cancel Christmas throughout the planet. It shall be a splendid funeral. And by the New Year, the World Economic Council will place me in command and then things shall really start to move."

James' little eyes squinted up at him for a long moment before turning to look out at the restless sea. He hung onto the rough seawall to keep from being toppled by the gentle night breeze and stared toward the dark waves.

"They will suspect you."

"There will be no proof. The last of the drug has just been dribbled into the sea. The change to your genetic code has already been registered in your electronic medical records, by a fine hacker who has, alas, suffered a memory loss due to some bad fish he ate. Very bad fish. You don't maintain paper files, so I'm safe."

Bryce leaned down to watch his face, but James was turned toward the night and he was totally in shadow. There was a long hesitation, then a twitch of his shoulders that Bryce could feel beneath his hand.

"But I do. I was most careful."

Not careful enough, old friend. He knew when James' was lying. It was for this that Bryce had risked telling him of his own death. The man was so naive that he hadn't banked hard copies against his future. So, Bryce's plan was going to go off without a hitch.

The Premier hung his head and his voice was a mere whisper against the susurration of the surf on the rocky cliffs below.

"What about my wife?"

Bryce glanced back to the surging dance floor. What an odd final question to ask before certain death. Given a chance, what would be his last request? Not about some woman, that was for certain. Though if ever there was one...

Even through the crowd Celia Wirden stood out. Her fountain of white-blond hair and the slender body beneath, shimmeringly not revealed by her gown of midnight-blue silk, did everything to distract from the brilliant mind that hid behind those green eyes.

The three of them had plotted together since they were young. They had thrown Parvati out of power and when it came time to choose, Bryce had forced the milquetoast James to puppet the Premiership for him. And the Premier needed a First Lady. A fine and elegant First Lady she had made. Perhaps it was time to take that gift back.

"She'll be taken care of, James. You don't need to fear for that."

James' shoulders squared slowly as the man looked a last time at the dark Atlantic. He took up his empty champagne glass from the seawall.

"Well, old friend. Seems that I am dry. Shall we go get a refill?"

"I am right beside you to the end of your days, James."

"Long may that be."

Bryce completed their old code, "Long indeed."

At the French doors, he checked James one last time. But he was filled with a bonhomie that even the finest politician couldn't invent. When he refilled the same glass and drank from it, Bryce knew the memory of the last few minutes was safely gone.

James was wrapped up into the flow of the crowd as Bryce waited upon the threshold. The broad squares of alternating black and white marble spread across the room before him like a grand chess board. The sycophants rushed to make what they could of the moment, shuffling like mad pawns, the tuxedoed livery of the government descended upon the wrong man. The short stature of the largest pawn of them all disappeared from view. Bryce would keep a close eye upon him, but not too close. Nothing must seem out of the ordinary.

He scanned the room. The ladies, those dragged forward by their men, and those abandoned in the sudden rush toward the Premier, glittered about. Their 1920s flapper costumes revealing both the wondrous and the corpulent with an equal lack of sympathy. But they too were all either carefully watching the rush to the Premier, or carefully not watching.

There were just four who were watching the Premier's Right Hand instead. His Captain of the guard, meticulous in his waiter's outfit, was nonchalantly poised to strike from his corner like a steadfast rook. The general commander of the World Economic Council's forces waited like the good knight he was, not obviously aligned, yet always prepared to offer surprise support from unexpected quarters.

Celia Wirden glittered like the queen that she was. The tight silk revealed a mature woman who had grown into her body the way a yacht grows into a World Cup racer. Her movements could light fire without ever striking a match.

His body responded from the memory of that one tryst three decades gone, the same night he'd sent her to become James' first lady. Her green eyes assessed him carefully from her position far across the room near the small orchestra. A chandelier blossomed above her in a font of crystal as if it had bloomed for her alone.

And off to the side, behind the piano, hid a single junior pawn. Without even the boy being aware, Bryce had been moving him across the board, square by careful square. Perhaps it was time to move the lad one step closer to the far side of the board, where he too would become powerful. Together, many things could be achieved. He would kill the king, take the queen, and create a prince.

Yes. It was time for the next move.

———

Keep reading at fine retailers everywhere.
The Nara Reaction
...and don't forget that review. It really helps me out.

ABOUT THE AUTHOR

M.L. Buchman started the first of over 60 novels, 100 short stories, and a fast-growing pile of audiobooks while flying from South Korea to ride his bicycle across the Australian Outback. Part of a solo around the world trip that ultimately launched his writing career in: thrillers, military romantic suspense, contemporary romance, and SF/F.

Recently named in *The 20 Best Romantic Suspense Novels: Modern Masterpieces* by ALA's Booklist, they have also selected his works three times as "Top-10 Romance Novel of the Year." NPR and B&N listed other works as "Best 5 of the Year."

As a 30-year project manager with a geophysics degree who has: designed and built houses, flown and jumped out of planes, and solo-sailed a 50' ketch, he is awed by what's possible. More at: www.mlbuchman.com.

Other works by M. L. Buchman: (* - also in audio)

Thrillers

Dead Chef
Swap Out!
One Chef!
Two Chef!

Miranda Chase
Drone*
Thunderbolt*
Condor*

Romantic Suspense

Delta Force
Target Engaged*
Heart Strike*
Wild Justice*
Midnight Trust*

Firehawks
MAIN FLIGHT
Pure Heat
Full Blaze
Hot Point*
Flash of Fire*
Wild Fire
SMOKEJUMPERS
Wildfire at Dawn*
Wildfire at Larch Creek*
Wildfire on the Skagit*

The Night Stalkers
MAIN FLIGHT
The Night Is Mine
I Own the Dawn
Wait Until Dark
Take Over at Midnight
Light Up the Night
Bring On the Dusk
By Break of Day

AND THE NAVY
Christmas at Steel Beach
Christmas at Peleliu Cove
WHITE HOUSE HOLIDAY
Daniel's Christmas*
Frank's Independence Day*
Peter's Christmas*
Zachary's Christmas*
Roy's Independence Day*
Damien's Christmas*
5E
Target of the Heart
Target Lock on Love
Target of Mine
Target of One's Own

Shadow Force: Psi
At the Slightest Sound*
At the Quietest Word*

White House Protection Force
Off the Leash*
On Your Mark*
In the Weeds*

Contemporary Romance

Eagle Cove
Return to Eagle Cove
Recipe for Eagle Cove
Longing for Eagle Cove
Keepsake for Eagle Cove

Henderson's Ranch
Nathan's Big Sky*
Big Sky, Loyal Heart*
Big Sky Dog Whisperer*

Love Abroad
Heart of the Cotswolds: England
Path of Love: Cinque Terre, Italy

Other works by M. L. Buchman:

Contemporary Romance (cont)

Where Dreams
Where Dreams are Born
Where Dreams Reside
Where Dreams Are of Christmas
Where Dreams Unfold
Where Dreams Are Written

Science Fiction / Fantasy

Deities Anonymous
Cookbook from Hell: Reheated
Saviors 101

Single Titles
The Nara Reaction
Monk's Maze
the Me and Elsie Chronicles

Non-Fiction

Strategies for Success
Managing Your Inner Artist/Writer
Estate Planning for Authors*
Character Voice
Narrate and Record Your Own
Audiobook*

Short Story Series by M. L. Buchman:

Romantic Suspense

Delta Force
Delta Force

Firehawks
The Firehawks Lookouts
The Firehawks Hotshots
The Firebirds

The Night Stalkers
The Night Stalkers
The Night Stalkers 5E
The Night Stalkers CSAR
The Night Stalkers Wedding Stories

US Coast Guard
US Coast Guard

White House Protection Force
White House Protection Force

Contemporary Romance

Eagle Cove
Eagle Cove

Henderson's Ranch
Henderson's Ranch*

Where Dreams
Where Dreams

Thrillers

Dead Chef
Dead Chef

Science Fiction / Fantasy

Deities Anonymous
Deities Anonymous

Other
The Future Night Stalkers
Single Titles

SIGN UP FOR M. L. BUCHMAN'S NEWSLETTER TODAY

www.ingramcontent.com/pod-product-compliance
Lightning Source LLC
Chambersburg PA
CBHW050914120626
46552CB00004B/1569